WHEN THE WIND STOPS

by **CHARLOTTE ZOLOTOW**
Pictures by **HOWARD KNOTTS**

An Ursula Nordstrom Book

HARPER & ROW, PUBLISHERS
New York / Evanston / San Francisco / London

WHEN THE WIND STOPS

Text copyright © 1962 by Charlotte Zolotow
Illustrations copyright © 1975 by Howard Knotts

Library of Congress Catalog Card Number: 74–2635
Trade Standard Book Number: 06–026971–5
Harpercrest Standard Book Number: 06–026972–3

JE

For
Eli Malachy Dunn Dapolonia
and
Blair Worthington Will
Bryce Morgan Will
Whitney Amanda Will
Brant Curtis Will

The great bright yellow sun had shone all
day, and now the day was coming to an end.
The light in the sky changed from blue to

pink to a strange dusky purple. The sun
sank lower into the long glowing clouds.
The little boy was sorry to see the day end.

It had been a good one.
He and his friend had played in the garden.
There had been icy lemonade in
the afternoon, which they drank
under the pear tree.

When they were tired, they lay down
in the grass and felt the sun on them,
warm and soft, like a sleepy cat resting.
And the little boy's father
read him a story on the porch
before he went to bed.

Now his mother came to tuck him in.
"Why does the day have to end?" he asked her.
"So night can begin," she said. "Look out there."
High in the darkening sky,
behind the branches of the pear tree,
the little boy could see a pale sliver of moon.
"That is the night beginning," his mother said,
"with moon and stars and darkness and quiet
for you to have sweet dreams in."

"But where does the sun go," asked the
little boy, "when the day ends?"
"The day doesn't end," said his mother. "It
begins somewhere else. The sun will
be shining there when night begins here.
Nothing ends. It only begins in another
place or in a different way."

"Everything?" asked the little boy.
"Everything," said his mother.

11

The little boy got back into bed and
his mother sat beside him.
"Where does the wind go when it stops?" he asked.

"It blows away to make the trees dance
somewhere else."

"Where does the dandelion fluff go
when it blows away?"
"It carries the seed for new dandelions
to someone's lawn."

14

"Where does the road go
when it gets out of sight?"
"To another little boy who sees it
begin in the distance."

15

"Where does the mountain go after the top?"

"Down to where the valley begins."

"Where do waves go when they break on the sand?"
"Sucked back to the sea into new waves."

"Where do ships go when they sail away?"
"Over the horizon to another harbor."

"When the storm is over, where does the rain go?"
"Into clouds to make other storms."

20

"And where do the clouds go when they move across the sky?"
"To make shade somewhere else."

21

"What happens to a train when it goes in the tunnel?"

"It comes out on the other side and goes to new towns."

"And the leaves in the forest when they turn color
and fall?"

"They go back into the ground and feed new trees
with new leaves."

"But when those leaves fall," the little boy said,
"it is the end of autumn."

"Yes," said his mother. "The end of autumn
is when the winter begins."

"And the end of winter?" asked the little boy.

"The end of winter, when the snow melts and the

birds come back, is the beginning of spring," his
mother said.

"It really does go on and on,"
the little boy said. "Nothing ends."
He looked out at the sky. The sun was
gone completely. The lovely pink clouds
had disappeared. The sky was dark and
purple-black. High in the branches of the
pear tree, there was a thin new moon.

"Today is over," his mother said,
"it's time to sleep.
And tomorrow morning the moon will be
beginning a night far away,
and the sun will be here,

          beginning a new day."